WITHDRAWN

Timbuktu

From KALAMAZOO to TIMBUKTU!

Harriet Ziefert

Paintings by Tanya Roitman

BLUE APPLE BOOKS

Text copyright © 2005 by Harriet Ziefert
Pictures copyright © 2005 by Tanya Roitman
All rights reserved. CIP Data is available.
Published in the United States 2005 by Blue Apple Books
515 Valley Street, Maplewood, N.J. 07040
www.blueapplebooks.com
Distributed in the U.S. by Chronicle Books

First Edition
Printed in China
ISBN: 1-59354-091-4
1   3   5   7   9   10   8   6   4   2

Here you are in Kalamazoo!

Millie and Mike in Kalamazoo
Were restless and wondered what to do.

Let's canoe to Timbuktu!

Said Millie to Mike, "I have a notion.
Let's pretend to cross the ocean."

You're pedaling to Timbuktu!

Said Mike to Millie, "Your plan sounds batty.
Let's make a call to Grandma Hattie.

She's got a bicycle built for two,
So we can pedal to Timbuktu."

The bike broke down in North Dakota,
So they stopped for an ice cream soda.

Millie said, "Don't make a fuss.
If we run fast, we can catch the bus."

The bus blew tires in Butte, Montana.
Millie took out her red bandana.

A helicopter pilot saw Millie wave.
"I'll help that girl; she looks so brave."

The copter sputtered over herds of cattle,
So they parachuted into old Seattle.

They received a call from Uncle Mort,
"I'll send a canoe to the local port."

They set out across the Pacific Ocean
With cases of food and suntan lotion.

We're paddling to Timbuktu!

Mike yelled to Millie, "Whatever you do,
I'll enjoy my trip to Timbuktu!"

The wind blew hard; the canoe upset.
Mike said, "I'm not so happy getting wet!"

Millie waved at a big blue whale,
Who said politely, "Climb on my tail!"

Over the wide Pacific Ocean,
The whale sped on with streamline motion.

Whale sang harmony for songs they knew,
Until she got hungry . . . and tired, too.

Whale ran aground in sunny Hawaii.
Mike and Millie waved good-bye-i.

They watched a hula-hula-hu,
Then set off in a new canoe.

They paddled hard toward Zanzibar
Till Mike complained, "It's much too far!"

A sailboat took them to the African shore.
They ate and slept, then ate some more.

They hailed a camel with two big humps.
"Ride with me if you don't mind bumps."

We've finally made it to Timbuktu!

The sun was hot; cool oases were few.
They hoped the camel would see them through.

Timbuktu was small but pretty—
An ancient, historical desert city.

Said Mike to Millie, "I'm feeling sad.
I want to see my mom and dad."

Mike and Millie boarded a plane.
Kalamazoo was on Mike's brain.

The skies were clear; there was no delay.
Mike and Millie were on their way.

Here we are in Kalamazoo!

It's great to travel, great to roam.
But even better is coming home!

Kalamazoo